For my mama
(I love you)
&
For my papa
(I miss you)

CONTENTS

1. A Beginning, of Sorts 1
2. A Day of Introductions 9
3. A Day of Unusual Classes 17
4. A Search for Little Bear 27
5. A Monster Expedition 33
6. A Very Curious Tradition 41
7. A Fever Flower 51
8. A Very Grand Picnic 61
9. A Tiny Monster 71
10. A Trip to the Circus 81
11. A Star with a Tail 95
12. A Winter Flurry 103
13. A Merry Christmas 111
14. A Knock at the Door 119

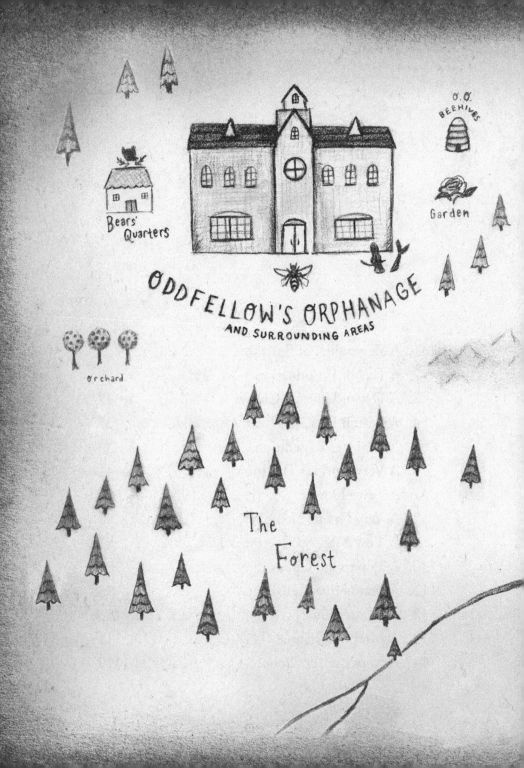

BEEHIVES

Garden

Bears'
Quarters

ODDFELLOW'S ORPHANAGE
AND SURROUNDING AREAS

Orchard

The
Forest

Fairgrounds

The
Great
Green
Lake

Here Be Monsters

N

ODDFELLOW'S ORPHANAGE

1

A BEGINNING, OF SORTS

"FLIBBERTIGIBBET!" sputtered the man with the blue-black beard as he awoke with a start. *There is another*, he thought. He leapt from his bed and put on shoes and an overcoat (which were always nearby in case of middle-of-the-night emergencies such as this).

There was a knock at his bedroom door. A lady's voice softly called, "Headmaster, there's been another."

The man swung the door open. The faint hall light revealed the owner of the lady's voice. She was dressed in a nightgown, topped by a fur-collared cape. The lady laughed at the headmaster's messy hair and his mismatched shoes. Her own red hair was neatly pinned up in a soft bun.

The man looked down at his feet and grumbled, "This is no

time to worry over shoes, Professor Stella!" With that, they both raced down the dark and quiet hallways of the orphanage and burst outside into the cool night air, followed only by their flickering shadows.

On the cobblestone driveway, a carriage waited. Like everything else in the orphanage, the carriage was rather unusual. Waiting in front of the carriage, where horses would usually be, were two large black bears. A young man stopped fiddling with the bears' harnesses and opened the carriage door for the professor and the headmaster.

"There's been another, I presume?" the young man asked.

"Yes, Hank, the message just came through," the lady replied as she and the headmaster climbed into the carriage.

Hank spoke quietly to the bears. They nodded their great furry heads and padded down the drive. As they got closer to the road, the bears' pace quickened, until off they bounded into the inky night.

Hank watched the carriage become smaller and smaller as it wound down the road.

Inside the carriage, Professor Stella nestled into the collar of her cape, pulled it snugly around her, and closed her eyes. The headmaster looked out the window into the twinkling night.

WHEN the bear-drawn carriage returned to the orphanage, the sun was creeping over the hills. Inside the carriage with the headmaster and the professor was a lump wrapped in a faded patchwork quilt. The lump shook off the quilt. There sat a little girl with white hair in two braids and pale blue eyes.

The girl looked around. In the seat across from her was a big man with a blue-black beard, a scarlet overcoat, and shoes that didn't match. Beside her was a lady with red hair and a fur-collared cape of the deepest blue. Both grown-ups were breathing gentle sleep breaths.

The little girl peered out of the carriage and saw two bears lumbering quickly ahead, pulling the carriage through patches of twisting trees and over hills dotted with early blooms. The bears slowed to a loping walk as an enormous house appeared.

The enormous house was made of brick and was surrounded by a garden of monsters. The little girl grabbed Professor Stella's shoulder and shook her awake.

"What is it?" the professor asked sleepily, squinting as her eyes adjusted to the light.

The girl waved wildly at the monsters going by outside the carriage.

Professor Stella laughed. "Oh! They're not real, don't worry. They are made of bushes and trees."

The girl looked carefully out the window. She saw that each monster was, in fact, a plant trimmed to look like a creature. There was everything from a sea serpent rising out of the grass to a towering mermaid.

The carriage came to a sudden stop in front of the steps to

the great house. The bears let out small roars to announce their return. These awoke the headmaster. He stretched his arms and said drowsily, "Home again, home again, jiggety-jig."

The door to the orphanage swung open. Hank came out as the professor stepped from the carriage. "Welcome back, Professor Stella," he said.

"Thank you, Hank," replied the professor as she held out her hand for the white-haired girl.

The girl took the professor's hand and jumped lightly onto the cobblestone drive.

"And welcome to you . . ." Hank paused, looking down at the small girl, who was shyly fidgeting with her white braids.

She didn't speak, but fished a yellow pencil and a scrap of paper from her pocket. She wrote on the paper and held it up.

Hank smiled. "Welcome to Oddfellow's Orphanage, Delia."

The headmaster jumped down from the carriage. Delia looked up at him. "And I am Headmaster Oddfellow Bluebeard," he said. "We are happy to have you with us, Miss Delia. I hope you will find that you belong here." He held out a hand that was really more like a paw.

Delia took his hand in her own small white one.

Hank unharnessed the bears and led them away. The headmaster, Professor Stella, and Delia climbed the steps to the orphanage. Inside, they had a breakfast of tea and toast before anyone else was even awake.

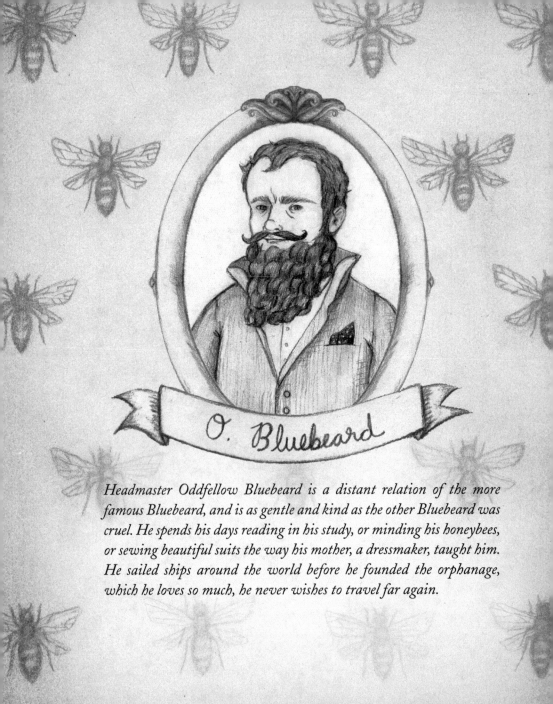

O. Bluebeard

Headmaster Oddfellow Bluebeard is a distant relation of the more famous Bluebeard, and is as gentle and kind as the other Bluebeard was cruel. He spends his days reading in his study, or minding his honeybees, or sewing beautiful suits the way his mother, a dressmaker, taught him. He sailed ships around the world before he founded the orphanage, which he loves so much, he never wishes to travel far again.

2

A DAY OF INTRODUCTIONS

FULL of toast and jam, Delia fell back to sleep right at the big wooden table. The three grown-ups didn't wake her, knowing that she'd be awakened soon enough.

They were right. Delia awoke to the sound of dozens of feet running overhead. She looked up nervously as the footsteps grew closer and closer, until the dining room was filled with a noisy parade of new faces. The parade soon sorted itself into separate children in painted chairs at the long table.

The dining room had smooth wooden floors and cream-colored walls. Sunlight streamed through the tall windows. Cooks in striped aprons carried in trays of fruit, little cups of eggs, baskets of breads, glasses of milk, and pots of tea.

The moment was so busy with the business of buns and buttered toast that no one noticed a new person at the table.

Then, all at once, they did.

Orphans and grown-ups alike stared at Delia, and Delia stared back at the peculiar group. There were more people than Delia could take in, but seated around her was a group she couldn't help but notice. A little hedgehog wearing a vest, who was attempting to eat an apple and a muffin at the same time.

A girl with shiny black hair, who had a yellow bird sitting on her shoulder. A girl whose arms and legs were covered in blue tattoos. A boy with acorn-brown hair, glasses, and a great many badges covering his sweater. And, strangest of all, a small boy who had an onion for a head!

The onion-headed boy politely said, "Hello."

Delia was looking for her scrap of paper on which to write "Hello" back, when Professor Stella appeared with a pocket-

sized red notebook on a long loop of string. Delia put the string around her neck, then fished the yellow pencil from her pocket. She turned to the first page of the notebook and wrote on it.

Then (because it would've used up far too many pages in the new notebook) Professor Stella introduced Delia to the other children her age and asked each of them to introduce themselves in turn. Delia listened carefully to the names and tried to remember them.

The hedgehog was Hugo. The girl with shiny black hair and green eyes was Ava. The girl with tattoos was Imogen. The boy with the sweater covered in badges was Daniel. A boy with blond hair and freckles was Felix. A round boy whose face was mostly hidden behind a book was Tom. Twin girls with golden curls were Lucy and Louise. The little onion-headed boy was Ollie.

After Ollie introduced himself, he said, "Would you like to hear a joke?" As Delia nodded, a funny barking noise came from outside the dining room. The barking was followed by a small roar and an even bigger bellow.

Just as Delia was starting to feel worried, Ollie turned to her, beaming. "It's Boris and Greta and the baby!" he said excitedly.

Delia tilted her head and gave him a quizzical look.

Just then, the door burst open and Hank's tenor voice rang out: "May I present . . . Oddfellow's Dancing Marvels!"

In came a family of black bears, tumbling and stumbling and making a racket. There was a big papa bear, very like the

two bears who had pulled the carriage. ("Boris," said Ollie.) Then came a smaller mama bear with a green ribbon around her neck. ("Greta," said Ollie.) And behind them came a very clumsy, very little bear cub. He barked and pawed at his mother and galloped about the room like an especially furry small dog. ("And *he's* just called the baby," Ollie said with a shrug.)

Hank followed the bears and clapped twice. Lucy and Louise ran to the old piano in the corner and began to play a waltz.

At the sound of the claps and the out-of-tune waltz, the bears formed a line from biggest to smallest. Then they began to dance. They stood on one foot and spun around in circles. They shifted from one foot to the other, swaying. Finally, Boris the papa bear and Greta the mama bear began to waltz, just like two grown-up people.

The baby bear, looking a little left out, wandered toward Delia.

As he reached her, he did a somersault and landed at her feet. The little bear stood, the top of his head reaching Delia's shoulder. He bowed clumsily. And Delia thought it was only polite to bow back. So she stood and bowed. Then she and the bear cub gazed at each other. Looking into the cub's bright black eyes, Delia felt a flicker of understanding.

It occurred to her that she had something in common with the bear: neither of them spoke—at least, not in the ordinary way.

Delia offered the cub a small piece of toast with honey. He ate it right up. The two stood quietly for a moment, speaking with their eyes. Delia knew that the little bear was saying something nice to her, and she tried her best to say something nice back to him.

Then came another sharp *clap! clap!* Hank said, "Thank you, bears, for welcoming our new student. Now it is time for breakfast!" With that, all three bears formed a line and, following Hank, bounded from the dining room.

Ava

One winter evening, Oddfellow Bluebeard heard a tiny knock at the door. Upon opening it, he found a girl with jet-black hair who was scarcely bigger than a small fire hydrant. She was shivering and clutching a birdcage that held three finches. The tiny girl called Ava (according to the scrap of paper pinned to her sweater) has grown much taller in her time at Oddfellow's. Her hair remains shiny black, and her eyes remain the same green pools that first peered up at the headmaster when she and her birds appeared so mysteriously many years before.

3
A DAY OF UNUSUAL CLASSES

BREAKFAST ended, and the children went to classes.

At Oddfellow's Orphanage, *nothing* was ordinary—for better or worse. This included the three classes the younger children attended every day. At other schools, students usually study things like math, reading, and science, but Oddfellow Bluebeard had rather different ideas about what subjects the children should learn, as Delia was about to find out.

Black-haired Ava walked Delia to each classroom, which was very helpful. The first class was F. T. Studies, which was all about fairy tales and folktales. This class was taught by Professor Flockheart, who was plump and rosy, with light gray hair. She welcomed the children from atop a stepladder, where she was searching the dusty bookshelves. Delia looked around at the cozy classroom, full of painted murals of fairy-tale scenes. She smiled.

Once everyone had settled down into their desks and Professor Flockheart had found Delia a rather scraggly set of books bound in green leather, the class began. They opened to the story of "Little Red Riding Hood," which was illustrated with lovely pictures. The children took turns reading aloud.

Midway through the story, the tattooed girl, Imogen, asked Professor Flockheart, "How could Little Red Riding Hood believe that a wolf in a bonnet was her grandmother?"

"Perhaps she needed glasszes," Professor Flockheart replied, which made everyone laugh.

Delia half smiled, and read along silently as the other children took their turns. She grew more nervous as her turn got closer. When her turn came, Delia looked up at the professor and, covering her lips with her small white hand, shook her head.

"I know, dear. Never to worry," Professor Flockheart said, and began to read aloud herself.

Class ended just before the woodsman arrived with his ax.

NEXT there was a class in cryptozoology, which is the study of mysterious and possibly imaginary animals. This class was taught by Professor Silas, the youngest of the professors. He had messy red hair and wore big glasses made of thick tortoiseshell. Professor Silas was well liked for his field trips and his wondrous laboratory, which was almost never open for visits (though those who had seen it declared it a marvel).

All of the animals they studied in Professor Silas's class were considered M.O.N.S.T.E.R.S.

Or, to write it out fully:

Mysterious
Or
Nonexistent
Subjects
Thoroughly
Examined
Really
Scientifically

(Though very few of the creatures were actually monstrous.)

That day, the class began a brand-new section about M.O.N.S.T.E.R.S. of the Lakes and Seas. Professor Silas was very excited about this particular area of study. He whistled as he passed out a new book to each child. Then he went to his desk and stood on his chair.

"My dearest class," he began, "today we will learn about the monsters that live in the lake and the sea. And I can't wait any longer to tell you what we will be doing tomorrow." He jumped down from his chair and wrote in big chalk letters on the board.

The room filled with excited chatter.

Delia wrote in her notebook and held it up to Ava.

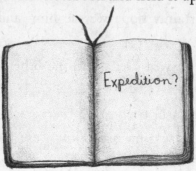

"An expedition is a field trip!" Ava explained.

"And where, you might ask, will we go on our expedition?" Professor Silas said. "I will tell you: the lake! The Great Green Lake. There, we will go on a boat and look for the Great Green Lake Monster."

"Oooooooh," all the students said softly, their eyes wide.

Then whispers traveled around the room.

Ava explained to Delia that they had studied many M.O.N.S.T.E.R.S. in Professor Silas's class. They read about them and looked at pictures of them in books. They drew them and wrote reports about them . . . but they had never, ever *seen* one. Not in real life.

The whispers turned into excited questions:

"Will it be scary?"

"Will we really see him?"

"If we do see him, will he try to eat us?"

Professor Silas answered easily: "We'll be quite safe on the boat" and "I certainly hope we see him" and "I really don't think so."

At that last answer, Delia and the other students looked relieved.

Then the professor tried to get everyone to read from their new books, but it was no use. They were too excited to do anything but talk about the Great Green Lake Monster.

AFTER Professor Silas's class was lunch. Students and professors alike gathered in the dining room for sandwiches and glasses of milk. After a chocolate cookie each, they all headed back to class.

The last class of the day for the youngest children was Astronomy. Delia was happy to see that this class was taught by Professor Stella, who sat at her desk at the front of the classroom. This room was just as lovely as Professor Flockheart's classroom, but was darker and more dreamy. The walls were deep blue, and golden stars shone on the ceiling.

They began class with a poem about the constellations. Professor Stella stood in the front, leading the children (except for Delia, of course):

Ursa Major is the bear, Ursa Minor is her cub.
Draco, the great dragon, could eat them both right up.
Scorpio, the scorpion, might give an awful sting
To Pegasus, the flying horse, upon his mighty wing.

There was a knock at the classroom door. Professor Stella answered it and found a worried-looking Hank. They spoke quietly, and Professor Stella frowned as she closed the door. Then she turned to the children and said, "The baby bear has gone missing."

Delia looked up with a start from her doodles of star animals. Her heart dropped.

"Everyone keep an eye out for him, please. He is missing from the bears' quarters," said Professor Stella. "Now let's finish our poem."

Slowly, the children started back up:

Leo, that regal lion, how he loves to run,
Chasing Lepus, the white rabbit, and Cygnus,
*   the white swan.*
But all the creatures made of stars have one they
*   must all fear,*
For Orion, the brave hunter, and his sword are
*   always near.*

Ursa Minor has gone missing! Delia thought. The moment Astronomy class ended, she hurried to Ava with a note in hand.

Ava nodded seriously, and with that, the two girls went off on their search.

The Bear Family

The bears named Boris and Greta originally belonged to a mean, greedy man. He trained the pair to dance beautifully, but made them dance in grimy streets, where onlookers threw coins at them. One day, the man was shouting and thumping Boris on the head when Hank happened to pass by. Seeing how cruelly the man treated them (and knowing that Oddfellow Bluebeard would welcome the addition of two fine dancing bears!), Hank bought them. He took them home to Oddfellow's, where, several years later, their baby was born. Now when Boris and Greta dance, they are happy, and never afraid.

4

A SEARCH FOR LITTLE BEAR

AVA and Delia walked through the gardens, checking around the monster shapes made of leaves. Delia peeked under a dinosaur's long tail. Ava peered beneath the sea monster's coils.

"Little Bear!" Ava called.

Delia called the bear cub with her mind.

Delia and Ava soon discovered that lots of other people were searching, too. Daniel and the Golden Rule Society had climbed trees for a better view. Ollie and Imogen sat on the highest branches, where they could see the edge of the forest. The mama bear wandered about sniffing the air, hoping to pick up the scent of her lost baby. The papa bear roared, hoping his cub might hear him.

The sky was growing dark when Headmaster Bluebeard joined in the search. He carried lanterns, and his pockets were filled with bear treats.

Felix and Hugo joined Delia and Ava, and the little search party took a lantern into the forest. They searched and searched for the little bear until the dinner bell rang out.

"Maybe we should take a break," Felix said.

"I'm sure the little bear wouldn't want us to *starve*," agreed Hugo.

One by one, everyone headed inside. Everyone except for Delia. She carried the lantern through the trees, calling for the little bear in her mind. She remembered the way her own mama used to call her when it got dark. *Only* I *wasn't lost*, she thought.

The tree branches overhead twisted and came together like long, skinny fingers. Delia searched beneath them until she was so tired that she could barely lift her lantern. Finally, disappointed, Delia followed the glowing windows back to the house. She passed by the dining room, where chatter and good smells spilled out, but she was too sad about the little bear to be hungry.

A pretty lady in a crisp white nurse's uniform stopped her. "Hello there, I'm Nurse Effie. Where are you going by yourself, dear?"

Delia sighed and fished out her pencil, then wrote in her notebook.

The nurse smiled. "Do you even know where your bed *is*? Aren't you the one who arrived just this morning?" She took Delia's hand and showed her to the room where the littlest girl students stayed. Inside were six small beds in two rows. On a pretty brass bed was Delia's own quilt, which had been cleaned

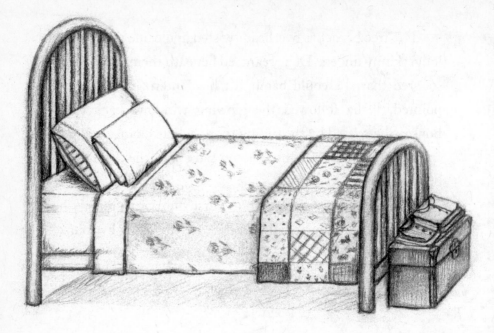

and pressed. On a trunk at the foot of the bed sat a stack of neatly folded clothes.

"You can hang up your clothes there, dear," the nurse said, pointing to a row of white wooden wardrobes lining the wall. Each of the wardrobes had a name painted in cursive letters on the door. One of them already had "Delia" painted in yellow.

"Good night. Have a nice sleep," Nurse Effie said, leaving Delia to change into her pajamas.

When Delia opened the wardrobe to hang up her dress, she heard a funny little barking noise and smelled something sweet. Delia looked down, and two bright black eyes looked up at her.

So this *is where you've been hiding, little Ursa Minor!* Delia thought at the little bear. *Everyone's been looking for you!*

The little bear stared sweetly back, then offered Delia a paw of honey from the jar in his lap.

Delia scolded the cub with her eyes. Then she smiled, took the cub's less-sticky paw, and led him downstairs.

Dinner was just finishing. One by one, everyone looked up at the white-haired girl in her pajamas and the honey-covered bear cub.

"Hooray!" Headmaster Bluebeard called out. "Delia has found him! Delia, you are our hero."

As everyone gathered around her, Delia *felt* like a hero. It surprised her that people she had only just met could make her feel so special.

Ava nudged her and said, "Good work! I'm so glad you're here."

"We are *all* happy to have you here," Hank agreed. "And I think that rascal bear's mama is happiest of all."

"Now tell us," said Ollie, "how did you find the baby?"

And everyone at Oddfellow's Orphanage waited patiently as the newest orphan wrote out her story.

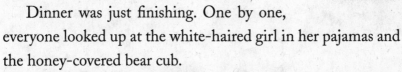

Prof. Silas

Silas was a gardener's son, but even as a boy he wanted nothing to do with his father's line of work. When he was old enough, he struck out on his own and became a student at the preeminent College of Crypto-zoology. After finishing his studies, he was surprised to learn that very few schools considered Unusual Zoology a necessary course of study—until he arrived at Oddfellow's. He can most often be found in his wondrous laboratory. It is rumored that he is responsible for the beautiful topiaries that surround Oddfellow's. (He has been spotted on more than one occasion with grass stains on the knees of his trousers!)

5
A MONSTER EXPEDITION

THE next morning, on the day of Professor Silas's expedition, Delia awoke to the sound of birds. She peered out from her blankets and tried to remember just where she was. She looked at the bed next to her and saw two black braids trailing over the pillow. *Ava,* Delia remembered.

Next to Ava's bed was a big brass cage, which held the chirping finches. Across the room slept two more little girls, each with golden ringlets ruffled messily on their pillows. On the other side of Delia slept Imogen, whose illustrated arm draped off the side of the bed. The other little girls soon woke up, and they all got dressed and headed to the dining room.

Breakfast was little stacks of pancakes that the cooks had

made into different shapes: hearts, stars, and tiny rabbits. After breakfast, Delia's class put on their sweaters and coats and headed outside. The sun shone brightly and the air was windy and crisp, as was proper for a March morning.

Headmaster Bluebeard was in front of the house with Professor Silas to help the children into a pair of carriages, each with two big bears hitched in front. Before they climbed into a carriage, the students picked up brown paper bags with their lunches from the steps.

Delia, Ava, Daniel, and Tom climbed into the first carriage, along with Professor Silas. Imogen, Lucy, Louise, Hugo (the little hedgehog), and Felix got into the second carriage. Last was Ollie, who ran outside, grabbed the remaining lunch bag, and jumped into the first carriage. Headmaster Bluebeard waved heartily as the carriages rolled away.

The ride went by quickly, and soon they arrived at the Great Green Lake. The children emptied out of the carriages and, led by the professor, walked down a long dock and stepped onto a boat.

The boat was large, but not large enough to dream of being called a ship. It was made of dark wood and was steered by a captain with a white moustache. The captain's only helper was his son, a young man with cheeks red from the wind.

The Great Green Lake was true to its name. It stretched far and wide in all directions. The water was the color of a dark emerald, and the waves that churned on the surface were capped in white foam.

The boat rocked as it cut through the water. It reminded Delia of the only time she had been in a boat before, when she was very little. She remembered being rocked by the waves while her papa sang her to sleep. Now she stood alone, the wind whipping her braids against her neck.

Professor Silas gave each student a pair of binoculars, and they spent the morning walking from one end of the windy boat to the other, searching the green waves.

They kept their binoculars held up to their eyes. They were too afraid to put them down for even a moment, in case that was the moment the monster decided to appear.

Professor Silas stood at the front of the boat. The wind blew his hair in front of his glasses. He consulted a map of the lake, which had notes and charts of the monster's habits and possible whereabouts.

"The lake monster can sometimes be lured in with a snack, such as a basket of fish," he told his students. "It's very lucky that I suspected as much and brought some fish with me!"

The professor took out little tins of sardines from his worn leather satchel. He opened the tins enthusiastically and tossed the contents into a small basket. The children held their noses at the fishy smell. When all the tins were empty, Daniel slowly lowered the stinky basket down to the water.

The children ran to the side of the boat to watch, in case the basket was gobbled up in one giant bite. Delia and Ava peered over the railing, hoping to catch a glimpse of fin or a flash of long neck or a flick of tail in the shiny deep water. They watched and waited, but the only shadows they saw were cast by the boat, and the only glimmers were of their own reflections in the waves.

After a while, they all grew tired. The basket of sardines bobbed up and down, still ungobbled.

"This is boring," Felix said, wrinkling his freckled nose.

Seeing the frowns and bored faces, Professor Silas cleverly announced a lunch break, saying, "The expedition will be put on hold while we eat our lunch and have hot cocoa downstairs."

The children cheered! Everyone galloped down the stairs to the boat's cozy cabin. The captain's son heated the milk to make their cocoa and ladled it into mismatched cups. Professor Silas spread out a quilt on the floor, and the students sat on it to eat their lunches. Soon all the passengers were warming their hands with a cup of hot cocoa and munching on a sandwich.

The only person who wasn't happily munching was Ollie, who sat frowning at his sandwich. "I hate cheese sandwiches," he said sadly. Without another word, he stood and started back up the stairs.

"Where are you going?" the professor called.

"To throw this sandwich overboard," Ollie replied.

"I'll eat it!" cried Hugo, but it was too late—Ollie was at the top of the stairs.

A few moments later, they all heard a small, sandwich-sized *plop*.

Then, a few moments after that, came a big, whooshing *SPLASH!*

"The monster!" Ollie shouted.

The children dashed up the stairs, followed by Professor Silas.

"Look!" Ollie called, waving.

There was the Great Green Lake Monster swimming swiftly away! His giant neck and tail curved through the waves, while his back rippled just above the surface. His body cast a huge shadow beneath the glassy water.

"I can't believe we saw him," the professor said, his voice quiet and amazed.

"Or that he likes cheese sandwiches," Ollie added, wrinkling his nose.

The monster and his shadow grew smaller and smaller until, even with their binoculars, the expeditioners saw only the great green waves.

Felix

Felix came to the orphanage after his parents were laid low by a poisoned cake that came as a gift from one of his father's business rivals. He hid in the kitchen cupboard when the ambulance came, and then lived alone (rather well) until neighbors spotted him sneaking home with a sack of groceries. When Oddfellow Bluebeard came to fetch him, the scrawny boy kicked and shouted and then promptly dissolved into a puddle of tears over the headmaster's great shoulder.

6

A VERY CURIOUS TRADITION

ELIA adjusted to life at the orphanage rather easily. Its strangeness soon became familiar to her, and even when she felt the most heartsick for her family, she never felt alone. She liked the other children, especially Ava, and the teachers were warm and kind. The cold wind of March turned to rainy April, which turned to sunny May. And suddenly, it was balmy June—which meant Haircut Day.

There were more than a few peculiar traditions at the orphanage, and one of the most anticipated was Haircut Day. Headmaster Bluebeard had decreed that a person really only needed two haircuts a year, and more frequent trims were just silly. So at Oddfellow's Orphanage, there was the Winter Haircut (on the first day of winter) and the Summer Haircut (on the first day of summer).

This was hardly a problem for the girls, who could just wear their hair tied back when it got a little longer. For most of the boys, it was a rather shaggier story. By the time November and May came around, they could often be seen swatting the hair out of their eyes, pulling it into a stubby ponytail, or squashing it all under a cap. And though there were sometimes messy attempts at late-night hair trims with dull school scissors, for the most part, everyone just got used to waiting.

When Summer Haircut Day arrived, breakfast in the dining room was filled with chatter. Delia thought making such a big deal over haircuts was funny. She loved her long hair, and it needed only little trims anyway.

"How short will you ask for?" Ava asked Delia.

Delia held up her finger to a few inches shorter than the end of her braids.

The boys sat a little farther down the table, and most of them (except for Ollie and Hugo) were shaking hair out of their faces as they tried to eat their muffins.

"I am going to have mine cut short," said Imogen. "So I am not too hot through the summer."

Felix looked grouchily in her direction. "You're going to look like a boy!" he said. "You already look weird, illustrated Imogen!"

Everyone looked startled at Felix's cross words.

"Boy, are *you* a grump!" Imogen retorted, sticking her tongue out.

The breakfast table was quiet until Ollie timidly broke the uncomfortable silence. "Maybe I'll ask Hank to snip off these little bushy pieces," he said, patting the top of his onion head.

Hank's usual job was minding the bears and circling the grounds on a great brown hare to be sure no scoundrels crept past the school's borders. But twice a year he was the orphanage's barber.

In observance of Haircut Day, classes were canceled. A striped canopy was stretched out over a big wooden chair Hank had lugged into the front yard. "Who's first?" Hank called merrily to the group waiting on the grass. His shiny silver scissors flashed in his hand.

"The headmaster should go first!" called Professor Stella, looking up from her book of old star charts.

The headmaster plunked down happily in the chair. "Oh, I do *love* Haircut Day!" he said. Then Hank went to work. The headmaster's hair was unruly and thick. Hank neatened it up in a big cloud of snipping. He also trimmed the headmaster's beard to its summer length. Delia watched as the feathers of falling blue-black curls grew into great piles on the ground.

The other grown-ups went next, ending with Professor Silas, whose dark red hair was clipped back from the overgrown state it was in. Then the children lined up for their turn. Delia got just a little trim, and Imogen got her sleek bob, which everyone (except Felix) admired. Ollie hopped into the barber's chair, and Hank carefully found a few (imaginary) hairs that he pretended to snip.

Daniel, being the leader of the Golden Rule Society at Oddfellow's, asked the headmaster if he should help sweep up the hair that piled the ground.

"No, no, Daniel!" the headmaster said. "We leave it—"

"For the birds to make their nests!" Ava chimed in.

"Exactly," said the headmaster, smiling.

"Let's take some to the edge of the forest, for the birds that live there," Ava said, turning to Delia, who sat rebraiding her hair, and Imogen, who shook her new bob happily. Delia and

Imogen nodded, and the girls gathered up the trimmings in their skirts and headed away from the group.

Suddenly, Delia felt a tug on one of her braids and heard a thick *sssniiip*. She whipped around to see Felix laughing as he ran away, holding one of her white braids in his hand.

Ava turned and saw him, too. "What is the matter with you?" she shouted after him.

Delia heard thunder in her ears. Her face was flushed with anger, and hot tears began to roll down her cheeks.

"Are you okay?" Imogen asked.

Delia nodded, sniffling.

Ava tossed her trimmings into the air and took off after Felix. Delia was too stunned to run, so she and Imogen followed behind Ava. Meanwhile, Felix had run straight into Professor Stella. Delia and Imogen joined the small crowd, where Professor Stella shook the white braid as she scolded Felix.

Felix shouted, "I don't care what you say. You're not my mother!" Then he ran toward the house.

The other children looked around wide-eyed, because such unpleasantness almost never happened at Oddfellow's. Professor Stella was equally stunned. "What in the world is the matter with him?" she asked. She looked around at the children's baffled faces. "Well, whatever it is, let's give Felix a little time to calm down from . . . well, whatever is troubling him."

After lunch, Daniel looked for Felix. He looked all around the house, then peered into the bears' quarters. Felix sat in the straw, spooning honey for the baby bear, who greedily gobbled it up. Daniel could hear Felix crying faintly.

"Felix?" Daniel said softly. "What's wrong?"

Felix wiped his face quickly on his sleeve and turned. "Nothing. I just hate Haircut Day." Daniel sat down beside him.

"Is that why you cut Delia's braid?" Daniel asked.

Felix sighed. "I don't know why I cut her braid. She's so quiet and nice. I don't know why I did it. I think I just hate this day because it reminds me of my mom."

"Why does Haircut Day remind you of your mom?" Daniel asked. "Was she a barber?"

"No, but she used to cut my hair," said Felix quietly. "She would pretend she was going to snip off my ear and laugh and . . . of course she would never do that. Snip my ear, I mean."

Daniel nodded in understanding.

Felix fed the baby bear more honey. "So when I feel those scratchy hairs prickling my neck, it makes me miss her."

The boys heard a rustling behind them. Delia stood there, and in place of her braids, she had two short pigtails.

"Did you hear all of that?" Felix asked.

Delia sat down next to Felix and took the honey and spoon. She turned to Felix, nodded, and put an arm around him.

Delia smiled at the bear. He made little barking sounds and licked honey from his nose. Felix leaned his head on Delia's shoulder as Daniel tiptoed to the door.

Nurse Effie

With all of the adventure and mischief to be gotten into, it's a wonder it took the orphanage so long to find a suitable school nurse. The headmaster searched high and low for someone with both a kind heart and a gentle hand, but when Euphemia Jane interviewed for the job, he was so dazzled by her crimson lips and faraway look that he gave her the job on the spot. Luckily for everyone at Oddfellow's (small and tall alike), all ailments from bumps and bruises to measles and mole bites are treated by a thoroughly clever and thoroughly soothing nurse. Her pretty rosebud lips and coffee-hued curls are just an extra nicety.

7

A FEVER FLOWER

WEEKS passed, and the air grew even warmer. Odd-fellow's halls were hot and bright from the great windows lining the walls. There were no classes in the summer, so the children spent all day playing. They picked blackberries in the woods, climbed trees, and read books.

The days' warmth stretched into the evenings, and every night Delia found herself kicking off her covers. Late one night, as she sleepily and grumpily kicked at the too-warm quilt, she heard Ava's finches chirping. Their chirps sounded worried, and Delia realized that she had never before heard them chirp in the night.

Delia climbed drowsily out of bed and padded over to Ava's side. She turned on the dim lamp. Ava's licorice-black hair stuck to her forehead, and her breathing was strange. Ava opened her eyes and just looked at Delia.

Delia thought of the way her own mama had always known what to do when someone was sick or hurt. She knew what bandages to use, what teas to make, and how to put on a puppet show to take your mind off a sore throat. But Delia didn't know what to do. She went back to her own bed and grabbed her pencil and notebook. She wrote a note, and then showed it to her friend.

A bad dream ?

Ava shook her head. "Nurse Effie," she whimpered.

Delia didn't want to leave Ava alone. She looked at the other girls, sleeping in their beds. Delia went to the next bed and tapped Imogen.

Imogen sat up and said something that sounded like "Whatsahmmmph?"

Delia pointed to Ava and wrote:

Going for Nurse Effie — Ava is sick !

Imogen's eyes opened wide and she quickly got up. "I'll stay here," she whispered. She went to sit on the edge of Ava's bed.

Delia crept as quietly as a mouse from the room and into the hall. Moonlight through the windows cast a shadow three times bigger than the girl walking quickly in her bare feet. She hurried to the east wing of the house, where the grown-ups'

rooms were. *It's a strange feeling to be awake in a house full of sleeping people,* Delia thought.

Furniture sat empty and the halls were ghostly still. The darkened floral wallpaper looked like a night garden that stretched on and on through the long corridors. At last, Delia reached a hall lined with a row of numbered doors, which led to the grown-ups' apartments.

Which is which? Delia wondered. She had no idea which door was Nurse Effie's! *I'll start at the first one,* she thought, and knocked softly on the door.

Delia heard a muffled exclamation, a great rumble, and then the sound of heavy footsteps. The door opened, and the headmaster peered out. "What's the matter?" he asked.

Delia scribbled in her notebook and held it up.

"Nurse Effie?" Headmaster Bluebeard said, completely awake now. "Well, we better scoot down there. On the double, Delia!"

Delia kept up with the headmaster as he walked briskly to the door marked with a brass number five and knocked. A few moments later, Nurse Effie appeared in her robe, her curls messy.

"Someone is sick, and Delia has come to fetch you!" the headmaster announced.

"Is it one of the other girls, dear?" Nurse Effie asked, looking down at Delia's worried face.

Delia nodded.

"Give me a minute," Nurse Effie said. She disappeared into her room and came back shortly carrying a large bag. "I'll take care of everything!" Nurse Effie whispered to the headmaster. "Don't worry!" Then she took Delia's hand, which made Delia feel instantly better, and they started off down the hall.

When they reached the little-girls' bedroom, all the bedside lamps were glowing and Ava's finches were chirping nervously. The other girls were awake now, and everyone was gathered around Ava.

"She's shivering, but she's burning up!" Imogen cried as Nurse Effie hurried to Ava's bedside.

Nurse Effie placed a thermometer in Ava's mouth. "I know just what's the matter." She turned to the ring of little girls. "I need something from the garden—something very important. Two of you will have to fetch it for me."

Delia, having made up her mind to be her bravest self, looked at Imogen, who nodded at her. They stepped forward.

"We'll go," Imogen said.

"Good," said Nurse Effie. "Do you know the plant with the little red flowers that grows in the back of the garden?"

The girls nodded.

"Good," said Nurse Effie. "Fetch me one leaf and one flower. Now hurry!"

As Delia and Imogen raced down the hall, they nearly ran right into a tall figure in the hallway. It was Headmaster Bluebeard. "I just couldn't go back to sleep," he said, his forehead wrinkled with worry. "How is the sick one?"

"It's Ava. We're off to fetch a flower for the nurse," Imogen said. "I think it's for medicine."

"Take my lantern," the headmaster said, placing it over Imogen's arm.

The girls ran lightly down the staircase and to the front of the house. When they opened the front doors, the air outside was inky black. Imogen lifted the lantern and Delia followed, so focused on their mission that she barely noticed the darkness. They made their way through the garden, all the way to the back row. Spying the small green leaves and vermilion petals they wanted, Delia pointed excitedly. She carefully plucked one flower and one leaf.

"Good eyes!" Imogen whispered.

Delia's hands were shaking, but she held the plant gently all the way to the house. Delia and Imogen hurried back through the halls and up the stairs. They burst through the bedroom door, where the headmaster had joined the group around Ava's bed. Delia placed the flower and leaf in Nurse Effie's hand.

Nurse Effie ground the plant with a mortar and pestle that came from her bag. She added drops of colored liquids from tiny glass bottles, and finally filled a small silver spoon with the red potion. "Here you are, dear," she said as she lifted it to Ava's lips.

Ava swallowed.

Delia wrote in her notebook and held it up to the nurse.

Will she get
well now?

Nurse Effie replied, "I think she will. I hope she will."

At that moment, Ava stopped shivering. Her eyes opened, and Delia could tell that Ava could see her. "What happened?" Ava asked, looking around.

"The worst Summer Fever I have ever seen," Nurse Effie replied with a tired smile. "And your friends brought the remedy."

Delia smoothed Ava's hair back and smiled at her friend.

Headmaster Bluebeard looked terribly relieved. "Hooray!" he said softly, and then added in a loud whisper, "And good work, Imogen! Good work, Delia!"

"She *does* still need her rest now, my dears, as do we all," Nurse Effie said. "So everyone try their best to get a little bit more sleep."

One by one, the little girls padded back to their beds. Delia closed her eyes and tried to sleep, but her covers were still too warm and she was just too wide-awake. Delia turned on her lamp and looked over at Imogen, who winked sleepily before falling fast asleep.

Delia quietly propped her notebook on her pillow. She opened to an empty page and drew brave girls and fever flowers until the first inkling of morning showed in the sky.

Hugo

Hugo, the little hedgehog, was orphaned at a very early age. Consequently, he became quite attached to a coarse-bristled scrubbing brush. When he was rescued by Headmaster Oddfellow Bluebeard and separated from his beloved brush, he quickly attempted to build a nest in the headmaster's facial hair, which in texture bore a slightly less striking resemblance to his departed mother. With time, Hugo has grown more independent and much larger, as his stomach seems to be bottomless.

8

A VERY GRAND PICNIC

ONE late-summer day, when the students were scattered away playing and the teachers were working in their respective studies, Headmaster Bluebeard sat in his study. *My, it has gotten very warm in here,* he thought, so he opened his biggest window. A cool breeze blew in.

The headmaster smiled as he looked out from his window over the garden and the grounds, to the woods beyond. The trees and topiaries were a lovely green, and the flowers bloomed in pale salmon pinks, whites, reds, and golds. The flowers reminded him of little cakes. At the thought of cakes, he had an idea that excited him so much, he couldn't keep from exclaiming aloud: "Picnic! Why in the wide world haven't we had a good picnic this summer?"

Since the headmaster wasn't very good at patiently putting ideas aside to think about later, he set to tearing about the orphanage like a spinning top. His first stop was the kitchen, where he merrily informed the two cooks to prepare for a picnic that would occur in three days. "Not just a picnic," he said. "A *grand* picnic! You have until Friday to prepare! Ha *ha*!" And he cheerily smacked the worktable, sending up a cloud of flour. When the flour settled on the table, Headmaster Bluebeard was gone.

The cooks turned to each other and exchanged a look that almost certainly meant: "Here we go again."

BY the end of the afternoon, the school was full of excited chatter about the Very Grand Picnic. The following days were full of making and baking (mostly in the kitchen) and choosing exactly what outfit was best for a picnic (mostly in the girls' rooms). Hank carefully strung fairy lights through the trees and filled the yard with picnic tables.

At last, Friday arrived. When the trees shaded the tables, everyone spilled out into the hot, sunny back lawn. Headmaster Bluebeard sported a very fine seersucker suit he had sewn the previous summer. The boys wore soft cotton shirts, and the girls wore airy dresses and skirts covered in polka dots and flowers.

The children surrounded the picnic
tables, which the cooks had piled with
platters and plates, each one filled with
a different delicious thing to eat.
Bunches of little sandwiches were
heaped in baskets lined with red-
and-white-checked fabric. Pies filled
with apple, cherry, blackberry, and
strawberry lined the tables. Beautiful
fruit was piled high in bowls, and small
jewel-colored cakes towered on glass stands. Sparkling pitchers
sat filled to the brim with fizzy lemonade and sweet iced tea.

It was so bright that Delia had to carry an enormous
parasol to shade her pale skin from the hot sun. She and Ava
traipsed over to the tables, fetching their plates
and filling them with little heaps of this
and that. Lucy and Louise selected all
the same things and ended up with
identical plates of treats. Tom was
attempting to serve himself a slice
of blackberry pie and read a book at
the same time. Hugo followed
behind, his plate covered in a small
mountain of cakes.

"Hugo! Save some for everyone else," Ava said to the little hedgehog.

"Oh, yes!" Hugo smiled and nodded. He chose one of the smaller cakes from his pile and put it back.

Everyone sat on quilts spread under the big trees and had their feast. The warm late-afternoon breeze gently ruffled napkins and hair. Robins chirped and hopped around close to Ava, and little gray squirrels darted around the picnic blankets, looking for lost crumbs.

A sharp *clap! clap!* came from across the yard, and everyone looked up to see Hank heading toward them. Behind him galloped Boris, Greta, and Delia's favorite, the little bear cub.

Delia noticed that the baby bear was a little bigger every time she saw him. He scampered toward the picnic blankets, looking for scraps of food. Felix knelt on a blanket holding out a honey cake, and the little bear ran to him and snarfled it up, while Hank treated Boris and Greta to handfuls of salmon sandwiches.

All that afternoon, there was happiness in the air. Professors Stella and Silas sat beneath a big tree, deep in their respective books. The cooks rested happily on the quilts, chatting and laughing. Greta the bear tumbled in the grass, chasing her rascal baby, while Professor Flockheart played her accordion.

The children took turns riding on the back of the papa bear,

who kindly offered short rides across
the yard. The headmaster gave
tours of his beehives, where the
bees were hard at work making
honey. Ava and Delia picked
wild strawberries, staining their
fingers and pockets red.

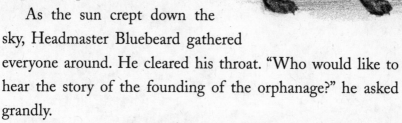

As the sun crept down the
sky, Headmaster Bluebeard gathered
everyone around. He cleared his throat. "Who would like to
hear the story of the founding of the orphanage?" he asked
grandly.

Quiet groans rippled through the group. Delia wondered why.

Daniel went to the headmaster, who stooped as the small
boy whispered in his ear. "Fabulous idea!" Headmaster Bluebeard exclaimed. Then he called to Daniel, who ran toward the
house, "We'll ready the stage."

When Daniel returned with a mysterious bag, Hank and
the headmaster had strung a line of rope between two trees and
draped two sheets over it. The children, grown-ups, and bears
waited excitedly on the quilts, facing the makeshift theater.
Daniel gestured to Felix, Ollie, and Tom, who disappeared with
him behind the curtains.

When the curtains parted (pulled by Tom), Daniel stood

sweating beneath a big brown overcoat. He wore a bushy blue beard fastened with string.

Felix walked onto the stage wearing a black coat and a crooked blue moustache. "Why, hello, Odd," said Felix. As an aside, he told the audience, "I am George Bluebeard, Headmaster Bluebeard's brother."

"Hello yourself, George," replied Daniel in a gruff voice. In his aside, he said, "I am young Oddfellow Bluebeard."

"Once Father is gone, I'll do what I like with my fortune! And you can do the same," Felix/George said angrily.

"I don't even want it! I don't know what to do with it," Daniel/Odd replied, crossing his arms. "But you, you will use it for something awful, I know it in my bones."

With that, Tom pulled the sheets closed and the first act was finished.

When the curtains opened again, Felix/George and Daniel/Odd stood next to a blanket and pillow on the ground. Resting on the blanket was Ollie, wearing a light blue beard that went nearly to his feet.

Daniel/Odd sobbed loudly into a handkerchief. "Father, please don't leave us!" he sniffed.

Ollie/Father Bluebeard coughed fiercely, which made his beard fly up. "It is time for me to go. Use your fortune well, boys. . . ." And with one last cough, Ollie dramatically dropped his head to the pillow and shut his eyes.

Daniel/Odd cried even louder into his hankie.

Felix/George didn't shed even one pretend tear, but announced, "With my inheritance, I shall open a big, giant factory! I will be rich! Rich!" And he ran offstage.

"And in that moment, I knew what to do with the inheritance because for the first time, I knew what it was like to be alone in the world," said Daniel/Odd, speaking to the audience. "I decided then and there to make a place for orphaned children and any lonely creature in need of a roof over its head."

Tom closed the curtains.

The real Headmaster Bluebeard cried into his handkerchief as the crowd clapped fiercely, though they had heard the story many times. Delia smiled, happy to hear the story for the very first time.

The sky was growing dark, and everything looked pretty and blue. Suddenly, tiny lights began to flicker on. Ava and Delia looked at each other. "It's Hank's lights," Ava said, looking around at the glowing spots.

Shaking her head, Delia smiled and scribbled something in her notebook.

"You're right!" exclaimed Ava.

Delia beamed.

The two friends looked up as more twinkling specks joined in. Soon all of Oddfellow's Orphanage stood silently gazing at the night air as hundreds of tiny globes flickered on and off, dancing in the trees and weaving slowly through the warm dark blue of the evening.

Daniel

Daniel was discovered by the headmaster when he was selling buttons on a sidewalk. Though most street boys his age found employment as pickpockets, Daniel, being honorable from the start, thought it amusing to pick the pockets of the thieves and return the stolen goods to their rightful owners. It was after reuniting an astonished and delighted Oddfellow Bluebeard with his wallet that Daniel found a home at the orphanage. Now Daniel is the president, student dean, and primary acting member of the orphanage's Golden Rule Society.

9

A TINY MONSTER

ON the first day the children returned to their classes in the fall, Professor Silas welcomed them with a surprise.

"Do you remember the last thing we studied before we finished our course on the M.O.N.S.T.E.R.S. of the Lakes and Seas last spring?" Professor Silas asked.

"Mermaids," Ava called out, and the other children nodded.

"Well, now that you're officially experts on that particular creature," said Professor Silas, "I have something I would like to share with you." The professor took his students to a small door that led from the classroom into his lab.

Professor Silas's lab was rumored to be full of strange specimens and scientific contraptions. Hardly anyone was allowed in, so it was a rare and thrilling treat when he let his class inside.

Grinning, Professor Silas took a key from his pocket and unlocked the small door. The children filed into the laboratory, staring up at the dusty stacks of books towering

over their heads. There were framed specimen boxes covering the walls, each one labeled neatly. Inside the boxes were curious small animals and plant specimens. As the children walked farther into the lab, light from the windows filtered through great glass jars containing ancient-looking fish floating in liquid, next to a glass-domed pedestal displaying a two-headed chick.

"This is kind of creepy," Ava whispered to Delia.

Delia nodded, but she couldn't stop looking around at all the strange things.

"This, class, this is one of the real prizes of my collection," Professor Silas said, pulling open a very long, narrow drawer. "Everyone squeeze in close to see." The children huddled around and peered inside.

"A beauty, isn't she?" the professor asked.

"She?" asked Felix. "It's a slab of rock."

"No, no, no!" replied the professor. "Well, really, it is a rock of sorts. But not just any rock. This rock holds the only known fossil of a mermaid. I call her . . . Pearl."

"Ooooh . . . ," murmured the children. Looking closer, they could make out the shape of the fishlike tail and the slender arms and neck and head carved into the rock by time.

Professor Silas nodded before gently pushing Pearl's drawer in place. Then he led the children back into the classroom, smiling contentedly. When everyone had settled into their desks, Professor Silas announced the new section: M.O.N.S.T.E.R.S. of the Mountains and Forests. The professor spoke merrily as he handed out new books: "First, we shall study the Yeti, also known as Bigfoot. Then we shall turn to the Great Horned Rabbit. And then . . ."

A breeze blew through the window and tickled Delia's ears. She gazed out onto the grounds. *The leaves are changing!* she thought. It seemed like it had happened overnight. She smiled—the fall had always been her very favorite time of year.

"Delia!" Professor Silas said, plunking a brown leather book onto her desk. "Come out of that daydream!"

Startled, Delia turned away from the window and nodded vigorously as she opened her book.

Later, as the children trickled out of the classroom, Delia walked with Ava, Daniel, and Tom, only she was walking so quickly, she kept leaving them behind. As she stood impatiently waiting for them to catch up, Tom called out, "Hey, what's the hurry?"

Delia took her notebook from around her neck and hastily wrote out:

It's FALL!

She held it up for her friends to see, hopping happily from one foot to the other.

"But fall's not going anywhere!" Ava said, laughing and pulling on her friend's satchel.

Delia's pigtails bounced as she trotted quickly toward the big front doors.

The children ran outside. Gusts of wind sent yellow leaves scattering and spiraling. All around was the magical feeling that you only get on the best autumn days. The nip at her fingers reminded Delia of the mitts her mama would knit to keep Delia's hands warm. She put her hands in her pockets and headed toward the red-leafed trees at the forest's edge.

Ava and Daniel followed, with Tom trailing behind, reading as he walked. Acorns bumped and cracked under their feet.

"Let's see how many acorns we can collect!" Ava called out.

They all bent and scooped them up. Daniel filled his pockets until they were big and lumpy. Ava filled her satchel until it rattled like a jar of buttons. Delia walked deeper into the forest, watching the ground for the prettiest acorns with the shiniest caps.

Her friends trailed behind at a distance.

Delia came to an enormous old tree. Its roots were dotted with orangey-red mushrooms, and the ground beneath it was soft with moss and fallen leaves. She stretched out onto the ground and spread her arms, fluttering them through the leaves the way children do in the snow. Delia closed her eyes and swooshed her arms. As she brought them back down, her hand brushed something—something that felt nothing like a leaf or an acorn.

Delia opened her eyes and looked over. Staring back at her were two dark, shiny eyes. A small brown rabbit sat right next to her hand, half buried in leaves. Delia slowly reached toward the little creature. It scampered through the leaves beside her arm and clambered up onto her chest. Delia smiled, looking at the rabbit's twitching nose. As her eyes moved upward, she noticed something very curious: a pair of tiny, perfect horns growing neatly between his smooth brown ears. Suddenly, the unusual rabbit turned its head sharply and froze.

Ava and Daniel walked up laughing, out of breath from an

acorn-throwing war, and Tom followed close behind. They saw Delia and the little rabbit and fell silent.

"Oh my . . . goodness," Ava whispered, her eyes wide.

"What is it?" Tom whispered, closing his book and stepping closer.

Delia sat up and gently placed the rabbit in her lap. She shrugged as if to say, "Who in the world knows what this little thing is?"

Tom, Ava, and Daniel sat, their legs crackling into the soft bed of leaves.

The rabbit peered up from Delia's skirts, blinking its bright eyes and nervously flicking its back legs.

"Should we take it to Professor Silas?" Daniel asked, lightly petting its head. It seemed to like this. The rabbit scratched a back foot against its horns.

Delia opened her notebook and began to draw the strange little creature.

"Oh, wait! I think I might know what it is," Ava said, opening her satchel. She took out the book Professor Silas had given them earlier that day. Biting her lip, she thumbed through the pages. "Himalayan Blue Monkey . . . no . . . Horse Fly (Rocking) . . . no. Wait! Yes! Here it is." Ava looked at the illustration in the book, and then at the rabbit on Delia's lap. "Hmmm . . . ," she said, frowning a little.

"So, what *is* it?" Tom asked.

"Well, I think this is it, but according to the book it's supposed to be bigger." Ava eyed the little rabbit. "Much, *much* bigger." She placed the open book on the ground for the others to see.

"The Great Horned Rabbit is very rare. It can grow to reach ten feet in length," Ava read aloud.

Delia wrote something in her notebook, then held it out.

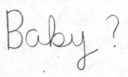

"A baby?" Tom asked.

Delia gestured to the illustration in Ava's book.

"Oh! A baby horned rabbit! I bet you're right!" said Tom.

"Should we take it back to school?" Ava asked Delia. She scooped up the little horned rabbit and held it to her face. It licked her nose with its tiny pink tongue. Ava laughed.

Startled, the rabbit wriggled from her hands. It dove into the leaves and darted away. The children watched it vanish into the forest.

The four stood up.

"Professor Silas will never believe we found a Great Horned Rabbit all by ourselves," Daniel said, disappointedly brushing leaves from his trousers.

"Maybe nobody will ever know about him," said Ava, half frowning.

Delia looked back into the trees where the baby rabbit had vanished, and then wrote something in her notebook.

Smiling, she held up the page.

We know.

The children smiled at each other, then headed back to the school, leaves crackling beneath their feet.

Ollie

Oddfellow's has made it a point to welcome young individuals of all stripes, which is how Ollie found a home there. After a particularly insidious strain of the onion blight known as the Smudge claimed nearly every member of his family, he ended up at the orphanage gates. One might expect that with so much tragedy in his young history, Ollie would be profoundly glum, or at least a bit cranky. Gladly, though, he is quite the opposite—perhaps because he knows of life's fleeting nature, Oddfellow's onion head is the jolliest of all students and is the only onion that will make you laugh rather than cry.

10

A TRIP TO THE CIRCUS

EACH year in the autumn, everyone at Oddfellow's Orphanage went to the circus.

"It's the bears' going-away party," Ava explained to Delia as the bear-drawn carriages wound down the road on the way to the circus.

Delia frowned. She scribbled a note in her notebook.

Why are the bears going away?

"Oh, don't look so sad!" Ava said. "They're not going away for good! They just go to sleep at this time of year, and stay asleep till spring comes. Our bears hibernate the same as wild bears."

At this, Delia's face softened. She wrote another note.

So we take them
to the circus?

The carriage jerked to a stop.

Ava smiled and said, "No, *they* take *us*."

Everyone—grown-ups, orphans, and the bear family—piled out of the carriages as the sun began to set. They gathered in a group outside a ring of trees. The headmaster gave each of the children a small red ticket and a little pocket money.

"Stay together in small groups, if you please," Headmaster Bluebeard instructed. "And when the show is over and done, everyone meet back here. Now, off you go—enjoy the circus!"

With Hank leading the bears, they made their way through the trees toward an enormous tent. It had faded red and white stripes and was capped with flags that fluttered in the chilly air. They walked around the giant tent and were greeted with an eyeful of curious sights.

Girls scarcely bigger than Delia and Ava wove their bodies into pretzel shapes, while elephants waved feathered head-dresses. A man as tall as a giraffe bent down to talk to a man shorter than Delia. Pretty ladies in jewel-colored robes looked into handheld mirrors and put on scarlet lipstick, while men in white makeup fed apples and carrots to satin-skinned horses.

Delia walked through the crowd with Ava and Ollie. It reminded her of a time with her family, one of the memories that would dash away and hide every time she got close to it. Delia was so busy watching the circus folk, she didn't notice when Hank and the bears disappeared into the tent.

Suddenly, a man with a curling moustache grabbed Ollie by the trouser pocket with his cane. Ollie came to a sudden halt, and Delia and Ava jumped back in surprise.

The man unhooked his cane and bowed. "We could use a fellow of your talents here in my show, young man," he said, looking at Ollie and twirling his cane.

"Talents?" Ollie asked.

"Well, your, ahem, unusually fantastic head, of course," the man explained.

Ava and Delia exchanged worried looks.

"No one has ever said it's *fantastic* before," Ollie said, beaming.

"Well, think about it. We would love to have you in our

family!" The man gave a wink and vanished as suddenly as he had appeared.

The sky began to grow dark, and a golden string of lights flickered on.

People coming to see the circus were lining up around the tent. Two tiny men in tiny black suits pulled back red velvet curtains that marked the tent's entrance. "The circus begins!" they called out, tipping their hats and bowing.

The audience made their way into the tent, which glowed inside like a magic lantern. Delia, Ava, and Ollie were giving the little men their tickets when they ran into Imogen, who had lost her group. Inside, they each bought cotton candy, and the four friends picked their seats.

Together they looked around at the great tent. On the walls hung painted pictures of circus performers with names like Fiona, the Fire-Breather! There was a big painted platform in the middle of the floor, with smaller ones around it. They were lit by brilliant spotlights.

The man with the curling moustache walked out grandly and stood on the red center platform. He raised a red megaphone to his mouth. The audience clapped.

"Ladies and gentlemen!" the man called, and the crowd hushed. "Welcome to Curioso's Circus! I, the official ringmaster, will lead you through our world of magical and marvelous sights tonight."

Music began to play, the lights flashed, and a parade began! There were tigers and lions, kind-eyed elephants and tumbling acrobats, silly clowns in pedal cars and beautiful, glittering ladies. They circled the inside of the tent to the music, and then the parade wound off the stage and out of view.

The ringmaster spoke again. "First! Our wild beasts from Africa—three majestic lions and two fearsome tigers with their brave tamer, the Amazing Bruno!"

The tamer led the parade of big cats onto the floor. They gave terrifying roars! The Amazing Bruno cracked his whip, and the lions climbed onto their small platforms. He cracked his whip twice, and the tigers (one white and one orange) rolled over onto their backs. The tamer scratched their furry bellies as if they were overgrown house cats.

The crowd cheered.

"That was my favorite part so far!" Imogen exclaimed, clapping as the lions and tigers were led away.

After the lions and tigers, there were acrobats, who swung from ropes that hung from the top of the tent. They swooped through the air and grabbed each other's ankles to make great chains.

Then came the tightrope walkers, who balanced on slender cables high above the floor.

Next the clowns swarmed the stage, and Ollie watched, entranced. The clowns raced after little dogs in ruffled collars, while the crowd chuckled. They tumbled after each other, tripping over their flopping trousers and silly giant shoes.

Ollie whispered, to nobody in particular, "I could do that!"

Ava heard him, and worry flashed across her face.

Next the elephants appeared, and the clowns scrambled out of sight.

"This is *my* favorite part," Ava whispered to Delia.

Ladies in sparkles, feathers, and glittering fringe rode on the backs of the elephants. The ladies did flips and twirled as the gray giants paraded across the stage. Some of the ladies juggled, some danced, and then a lady in a gown of silver blew a blast of fire into the air!

The audience gasped, and their applause rang out loudly.

The ringmaster announced the final act. "Tonight, my friends, we have a very special surprise treat for you. Tonight, and *only* tonight, I give you"—the tent was silent—"Oddfellow's Dancing Marvels!"

Out came Boris and Greta, dressed in beautiful satin ruffs. The music changed, and the mama and papa bear waltzed across the floor. Then Boris and Greta parted and held out their paws toward the baby. He wore a feathered cap and a satin vest and, to everyone's surprise, was riding a small bicycle! He

pedaled in a dozen speedy circles around his parents, then, at last, climbed off and took a dizzy bow. He got the biggest applause of the whole night.

Delia wrote in her notebook and showed it to Ava.

That was <u>my</u> favorite part!

IT was dark when the Oddfellow's party returned to their carriages. The headmaster counted everyone and came up one head short—one onion head, that is!

"Oh, no!" Ava cried. "Ollie's run off with the circus."

The orphans turned to each other in shock. Just as Hank and the headmaster were about to march back to the tent to find Ollie, they heard a scurrying sound coming through the trees.

"Ollie!" everyone cried out as he came into view.

"So you haven't left us to join the circus, my boy?" the headmaster asked.

"Of course not!" Ollie exclaimed, smiling. "I just had to try on some of those clown shoes." Then quietly he added, to nobody in particular, "I've already got a family, thankyouverymuch."

BACK, at Oddfellow's, everyone tumbled out of the carriages.

All the bears—the ones Hank unharnessed from the carriages, and the bear family—were yawning already.

"Looks like it's time to say good-bye," Hank said. "Or maybe good night. They need to get started on their long winter sleep."

Delia went to the bear cub. How tall he had grown since she had first met him! While he was still small as bears go, he stood almost nose to nose with her now. Delia looked into his sleepy eyes and told him silently what a good job he did at the circus. He blinked back in a way that made her certain that he understood. Delia flung her arms around him, burrowing her nose in his soft fur.

The other children

gathered around the bears, petting them and hugging them around their great, warm necks.

"I'll miss you, fella," said Felix, scratching under the baby bear's chin.

"Good night, you fine bears! We will see you sooner rather than later," called Oddfellow Bluebeard.

They all watched as Hank led the dark, drowsy shapes back to their quarters, where they would soon burrow into a mountain of blankets and fall asleep, dreaming of honey or leaping fishes or whatever it is that bears dream of, until the warm spring air woke them.

Prof. Stella

Once an orphan at Oddfellow's herself, Stella returned to the school under mysterious circumstances. Now she is professor of Astronomy and also serves as adviser to the student members of the Society for the Care and Appreciation of Dancing Bears. It will come as no surprise, then, to find that her favorite constellation is Ursa Major. On clear nights, she can often be seen dragging her telescope outside her window, as her plans for a grand observatory have, much to her dismay, gone unfunded.

11

A STAR WITH A TAIL

HAIL clattered on the windows of the dining room. The cooks had surprised the children with mugs of hot chocolate capped with small clouds of whipped cream to go along with their breakfast. Everyone was very happy to be cozy and dry inside, rather than wet outside (and with no toast and jam).

"Hot chocolate for breakfast!" Ava said, nudging Delia happily.

Delia drank it slowly, feeling it warm her up as it went down.

Hugo sat next to them at the breakfast table. He took an enormous sip of cocoa and set down his mug, wiping the moustache of cream from his lip. He was in the middle of asking for another mug when the headmaster strolled to the front of the dining room.

The room grew quiet except for the hail clicking on the windows.

"Everyone!" called Headmaster Bluebeard. "Professor Stella has something important to tell us!"

The professor sat at the teachers' table with her nose in a big blue book inlaid with gold stars. Upon hearing the headmaster's announcement, she peered over the book to see every

eye in the room on her. She closed her book and walked to the end of the long table.

"Good morning, everyone," the professor said. She cleared her throat. "I have something exciting to tell you—something that hasn't happened for seven hundred years but is about to happen again this very night!"

The room filled with murmurs. The children looked at each other, wondering what this seven-hundred-year-old thing could be.

"What is it, Professor?" Imogen called.

"A comet!" announced the professor. "The Great Comet will be seen in the sky tonight. That is, if the sky clears up."

THAT day, their Astronomy class, which was usually calm, was very lively. Professor Stella glided about the room, smiling as she answered the children's questions about the Great Comet.

"Is a comet made from the same things as a star?" asked Felix.

"Yes and no," said the professor. "One of the ingredients that make a star and make a comet is the same: gas. But stars and comets are very different, because a star is created from a collapsing cloud of gas. A comet is more like a great big dirty snowball, made of ice and rocks. Plus, a comet has a tail."

"A tail?" the children asked. "Like the tail of a cat?"

Professor Stella laughed. "Maybe a giant cat! The tail of a comet can grow to be many millions of miles long. That's longer than any road in the world. Can you imagine?"

The professor showed them big drawings that she had to unroll on the floor and told them stories about the Great Comets through history. Before the students knew it, class was over!

When the children left for the afternoon, the professor went to the window. The hail was still falling and the sky was still cloudy. Professor Stella's eyes were filled with worry. She frowned and turned to dusting her collection of miniature solar systems to distract herself from the disheartening weather.

Later that afternoon, the hail turned to an icy drizzle and finally slowed to a stop, but the clouds stayed stubbornly right where they were. The orphans played in the living room, warmed by a crackling fire, with frequent glances out at the dreary day.

Lucy and Daniel played checkers at a table, and beside them, Lucy's twin, Louise, was in a fierce chess match with Felix. Tom and Ollie were both reading on a couch— Tom a big clothbound volume from the library, and Ollie a comic book. Hugo, Delia, and Imogen lay on the floor drawing pictures, pencils and crayons scattered all around them. Nurse Effie sat alongside them, mending things and teaching Ava simple sewing stitches until dinnertime came.

At dinner, they had chicken potpies filled with carrots and potatoes. The pies were so good that, for a while, they kept everybody from looking out the windows. After dinner, the children stacked their plates up for the cooks.

The windows showed sooty rectangles of sky, so it came as

a surprise when Professor Stella appeared, bundled in her coat and holding her telescope. She asked everyone, including the grown-ups, to put on their coats and get ready to go out into the chilly night air. "You never know," she said.

Everyone gathered in front of the house, bundled in coats and scarves and mittens. It was windy, and the clouds moved quickly in the sky, showing occasional flashes of a white crescent moon.

With her telescope, Professor Stella searched for a break in the clouds big enough to spot the comet, but they were too knitted together to see anything. The children and grown-ups craned their necks skyward. The wind rustled through the dark trees, and Delia put her mittened hands in her coat pockets.

After a while, people began to talk and give their necks a break from staring at the cloudy sky.

Suddenly, the twins called out in unison: "I see it! Professor, I see it!"

Every head looked up. The clouds were breaking apart at their seams. Between the wisps of cloud was a glowing tail joined to a bright spot. It looked like something dashing across the sky, but it didn't move!

"It's like a big shooting star that's not shooting at all, but kind of creeping along," Lucy said, squinting.

"Or a dirty snowball," Ava whispered.

Delia nodded.

"I've never seen a snowball that looks anything like that," Felix replied, shaking his head. "I think it's really a great big star with a tail."

Professor Stella's face glowed as she gazed at the sky. "I've been waiting to see you for so long! I knew you'd come," she said contentedly. Everyone stared and stared for what seemed like hours, watching the clouds drift over and around the bright dash.

At last, the group scattered, and they all slowly made their way back to the house. Everyone went to bed very quietly that night. They washed their faces and climbed into bed, hushed with wonder at the sight of something new and marvelous in something as old and familiar as the night sky.

Hank

Hank arrived at the orphanage as a young man looking for a few days' work, but Oddfellow Bluebeard found him so helpful and friendly that Hank never left. During the day, Hank's most important job is to tend the bears and their quarters. His duties also include patrolling the perimeter of the orphanage, fixing things that are broken, and generally making sure that all is right and safe.

12

A WINTER FLURRY

A week before Christmas, a special feeling spread through the orphanage. Classes were canceled for the holidays, so during the day, the children practiced their Christmas play. Ava, Delia, Imogen, and Hugo paced the library rehearsing their parts. The twins practiced the piano accompaniment. Felix and Daniel helped Hank ready the stage, and Ollie and Tom painted backdrops and gathered props.

The children enlisted Nurse Effie (whose mending stitches graced many of their trousers and dresses) and the headmaster himself (also handy with a needle and thread) to help with the costumes.

In the evenings, Delia and Ava worked on making special presents for each other. This was tricky as it is very hard to make presents for people you are with all day long! The girls solved this problem by stringing a sheet between their two beds so they each had a makeshift workshop. The only sounds that could be heard (other than Ava's finches) were mysterious scissor snips and the rustling of paper.

For all the long days of preparations and excitement, Christmas Eve arrived rather suddenly. It announced itself with fresh snow flurries, and after breakfast everyone joined Hank on his search for the perfect Christmas tree.

As they all tromped through the woods, the cold air froze Delia's nose. Daniel pointed out two spotted deer, their bodies warmly brown against all the wintry white. The deer watched the procession of woolen winter coats as the children and grown-ups made their way to the grove of Christmas trees, the snow muffling all sounds.

Inside the grove, towering above the other trees, stood a magnificent fir tree. It was clothed in proud green branches, and everyone agreed it was the one that belonged at Oddfellow's. Hank made one swift cut with his ax, and he and the head-master hoisted the giant fir onto their shoulders.

Delia remembered her papa carrying a Christmas tree, smaller and more modest, of course. Delia pinched a sprig of needles, breaking them between her fingers, and the sweet piney smell filled her with warmth.

When they returned to Oddfellow's, it was late morning. Delia and Ava scrambled up the stairs to their room to finish their presents. They had been working away for hours when Professor Flockheart peeked in.

"They're making a gingerbread house in the dining room this afternoon," she reminded the girls. "And tonight we decorate the Christmas tree. Then Headmaster will do his annual recitation of the Christmas poem."

The girls finally finished their secret gifts just as the delicious smell of cloves and ginger reached their bedroom. They raced down the stairs and found Nurse Effie, Professors Silas and Stella, and most of the children gathered in the dining room. Delia and Ava found a place to sit as the cooks carried in big trays. One of the trays contained huge ginger cookies cut into squares and rectangles. The other held decorations and a great bowl of fluffy frosting as white as the snow that fell outside.

Nurse Effie showed everyone how to put the house together properly, and then the best part began—fancying up the plain cinnamon-brown house.

There were peppermint pillars, slabs of chocolate for shingles, pieces of cooked-sugar glass for the windows, gumdrop cobblestones, and sugars in red, pink, and icy blue. By the time they were done, everyone had eaten as many shingles and cobblestones as graced the house.

AFTER dinner, when everyone was dressed in their pajamas, the headmaster gathered them all in the living room to decorate the tree. The fire was crackling, and the tree stood grandly. Hank had covered it in strands of lights, and its branches were ready for decorations. Professors Stella and Silas brought in boxes of ornaments, and the children carefully unwrapped the glittering treasures wrapped in tissue.

Delia found a crimson glass heart and a small golden bird. The bird reminded her of Ava's finches, and she tucked it into her friend's hand. While the other children hung their ornaments low, the two girls stood on their tiptoes to reach the highest and best branches. When the tree was finished, the living room lights were turned off, and the tree lights were turned on. The tree was beautiful!

Delia smiled to see the heart and bird dance proudly near the top.

The headmaster settled into his overstuffed chair. He gazed about the room at all the dear faces, and his eyes misted over, twinkling in the light of the tree.

Everyone sat waiting expectantly, until suddenly, Ollie called out, "The poem, Headmaster. Will you say it?"

"Oh, yes, oh, yes. Quite right. The poem," he said, smoothing his beard.

"Children, this poem is called 'A Visit from St. Nicholas,' and this is how it begins. . . ." The headmaster took a breath. "'Twas the night before Christmas, when all through the house / Not a creature was stirring, not even a mouse. . . .'" Oddfellow Bluebeard recited the poem from memory, and at the end, he boomed out like Santa Claus himself, "Happy Christmas to all, and to all a good night!"

Merry applause rippled through the living room.

"And that is that, little ones!" said the headmaster. "Remember, the earlier you get to bed, the earlier Christmas morning will come."

The children made their way up the stairs to the third floor.

As Delia climbed into bed, she saw snow falling outside the window. She felt so cozy tucked in her bedcovers, she imagined she was a tiny girl nestled inside a warm matchbox. Delia heard the nighttime peeps of the finches and heard Ava whisper "Good night" before they all drifted off to sleep thinking of Christmas morning.

Ava dreamed she lived in a giant gingerbread house, and Delia dreamed she was small enough to ride on the back of a finch.

Imogen

Imogen comes from a long line of Illustrated Men and Ladies, though sadly none of them survived the winter of her seventh year and the particularly insidious strain of influenza that came with it. Having only one remaining relation, a wild-eyed grandmother prone to bouts of sleepwalking, she spent her eighth year lonely and nervous in a little white house on a river. One night, as the grandmother slept more horizontally than usual, Imogen tiptoed to a rowboat and drifted speedily on the current into the inky night. When the sun woke her, she found herself on the back of a big black bear, approaching Oddfellow's Orphanage.

13

A MERRY CHRISTMAS

IMOGEN woke the other girls by crowing, "It's Christmas morning, everyone!"

Delia and Ava sat up quickly, shivering with excitement. It was still dark outside.

In the room next door, the boys sat impatiently in their beds, listening for signs that anyone else was awake.

The house was perfectly still until the sun swept the shadows away. Then rustlings and grown-up voices were heard. In a snap, all the children were dressed, running downstairs carrying boxes and packages.

Ava and Delia carried their presents wrapped in brown paper and striped twine. Entering the living room, they both stared in wonder. The tree was circled with packages wrapped in dozens of

different papers. Delia and Ava added their two small packages to the mountain of presents. They oohed at the plump stockings embroidered with each child's name arranged on the hearth.

Lovely smells led everyone to a breakfast of cinnamon buns in the dining room, along with milk and coffee and tea. The children ate their buns in record time, and when the headmaster called out, "Well, goodness! Let's have Christmas!" the dining room emptied in a blink.

In the living room, Headmaster Bluebeard appointed himself and Nurse Effie as official Elves. They got to work passing out presents, and a great flurry of rustlings and tearing paper began.

Delia had a small mountain of gifts. She was so happy just looking at them that she didn't want to open them up.

Ava scooted over with her own gifts and squeezed Delia's arm. "Who could this be from?" Ava said, moving a present to the top of her pile. The tag read: TO: AVA, LOVE: DELIA.

"Oh!" Ava cried. "Where's the one I made for you?"

Delia shuffled through her presents and beamed as she held up a lumpy parcel with striped string.

The girls tore open their packages at the same time. They admired their presents in happy silence. In Ava's hands rested the little book Delia had made for her. It had a red paper spine and a crimson ribbon to tie it closed.

Finally, Ava opened it. Inside were drawings of sea monsters and horned rabbits, magic flowers and the circus, along with stories Delia had written about each adventure.

Clutched to her chest, Delia held a floppy black bear. He had glass-button eyes and a red nose. He was made of nubby wool that strongly resembled Ava's favorite cardigan.

"So you'll always have a little bear with you," Ava said, looking bashfully at the soft, lumpy doll.

Delia reached for the notebook around her neck, then instead wrapped her arms tightly around her friend, squeezing the book and the bear between them.

With the best behind them, the girls could open their other presents. Their stockings were stuffed with candy and fruit, and a new notebook for Delia, and bird treats for Ava. There were jars of the finest honey and windup animals from the headmaster; binoculars from Professors Silas and Stella, which could be twisted together in such a way as to create a telescope; copies of *The Little Mermaid* from Professor Flockheart; and pretty new blouses sewn by Nurse Effie. And from Hank, roller skates with thick leather straps that could be buckled on top of ordinary shoes.

THAT evening, they had a Christmas feast with an enormous turkey and a dozen side dishes.

After dinner, Daniel arranged the dining chairs into rows in front of the stage that had been set up in the dining room. Everyone except the performers and the stagehands sat down.

The dining room lights were dimmed and the little lights along the stage's edge lit up. Rustlings came from behind the curtains. The audience waited, looking at folded programs. Lucy and Louise began to play the piano, and the curtains parted.

On the stage were Snow White and Rose Red. Delia wore an ivory dress and had a wreath of white flowers circling her head. Ava wore the same, only in shades of vermilion and crimson. The backdrop was painted with a cozy wooden cottage.

The story was about two sisters and their poor mother (played by Imogen in a gray bun) who lived in a tiny cottage in the woods. One night, there came a loud knock at the door. When Delia/Snow White opened it, there was a brown bear (no one could tell who it was) shivering from cold. The girls treated the bear sweetly and let him sleep by their fire, until one day he disappeared as mysteriously as he had come.

The curtains closed for the second act, and applause filled the air. When the curtains opened again, Snow White and Rose Red stood in front of a lovely forest. The girls saw a little dwarf (played by Hugo). His beard was tangled in a tree branch, and the girls freed him by snipping his beard with a pair of scissors. But instead of thanking them, he screamed at them and ran off into the forest. The girls helped the dwarf out of two more scrapes and mishaps. Each time he was ungrateful and horrid and mean.

The curtains closed again to more applause. In the third act, the dwarf sat in the forest, polishing a heap of jewels. When Snow White and Rose Red came by him, he yelled at them to go away. Then, from offstage, a growl was heard, and in came the brown bear!

"Dear Mister Bear! Please don't eat me," cried the dwarf. "Take my jewels, and eat these wicked girls instead."

The bear knocked the dwarf to the ground with a single blow. Hugo lay there as still as could be, trying to play dead, even though the whiskers of his beard tickled him terribly.

The bear called out to them (in a voice trying very hard to sound gruff), "Don't be afraid, Snow White and Rose Red! It is your friend, the bear. That evil dwarf put a spell on me long ago." As he said this, the bear's fur began to fall to the floor to reveal Felix. "Now that he is dead, I am back to my princely self," Felix/the prince said, putting a golden crown on his head.

From offstage, Imogen's voice called, "And they all lived happily ever after in a castle surrounded by rosebushes of red and white. The end!"

The audience stood and clapped.

Ava, Delia, Felix, Hugo, and Imogen joined hands onstage and took a bow as the curtains closed once again.

"A Christmas gift indeed!" shouted Headmaster Bluebeard, his voice rising above the hubbub.

After the play, since there were no nearby houses to visit for caroling, they all sang Christmas songs around the piano. Finally, everyone made their way up the stairs to bed.

Exhausted, Delia and Ava flopped into their beds. One was tucked in with a little woolen bear and the other with a rumpled paper book, both happy and cozy as a pair of kittens.

Delia

Delia was brought to Oddfellow's late one night after her parents and younger sister were done in by bandits. The immigrant family, all albinos with the whitest hair and snowy eyelashes, was a traveling attraction with Captain Marvelous's Sideshow. Delia escaped by pretending to be a pile of laundry and, as she is very quiet, was quite convincing. The headmaster accompanied the police to the scene and found Delia hiding folded up in an enormous quilt, with one white braid trailing out.

14

A KNOCK AT THE DOOR

"ANYONE who wishes to stay up for the stroke of midnight is welcome to try!" Headmaster Bluebeard proclaimed on New Year's Eve, waving at the large clock on the dining room wall. "I always stay up to see the New Year come dashing out of the gate, and I welcome any company!"

Instantly, all the children made up their minds to stay up late.

Now, just a few hours before midnight, almost everyone was still awake. The dining room was lively with music from the piano. Professor Silas swept Professor Stella out of her chair, laughing. They danced across the wooden floor, a whirl of ginger-colored hair and swirling skirt. When they sat down again, both were flushed and laughing.

POP! POP! POP! went the New Year's crackers as children pulled them (only a little early). Small toys and paper hats fell out of the shiny cylinders. Everyone sat in the dining room wearing their silly hats and drinking fizzy drinks. Delia and Ava toasted with their glasses, practicing for midnight.

"An idea occurs!" called Headmaster Bluebeard. "Everyone stand up." He whispered something to Hank and Professor Silas, and together they pushed the dining tables to the walls. This created a big, open space in the center of the room.

"Fetch your roller skates, children!" said the headmaster.

Delia and Ava exchanged looks.

"We can skate inside? Really?" Ava called out.

"Only on New Year's Eve, Miss Ava!" Oddfellow Bluebeard replied merrily.

The children thundered up the stairs to get their skates. A few moments later, the dining hall was filled with the whooshing of dozens of little wheels zooming around the room. Skating made Delia very nervous, and she wobbled along slowly until Ava and Imogen sailed up behind her. They each linked an arm into one of Delia's and pulled her smoothly along.

As the night wore on, little skaters plunked down into chairs until the last set of wheels whirred to a stop. The hands of the clock inched closer to midnight. Some sleepy children and grown-ups made their way upstairs for bed, too tired to care about waiting for the clock to strike twelve. Finally, the only people left among the paper hats and empty chairs were Nurse Effie, Delia, Ava, Daniel, and Headmaster Bluebeard.

"Well, we five night owls will ring in the New Year together!" said the headmaster, smiling.

The clock's hands ticked closer and closer to midnight. When only a sliver of space remained between the little hand and the twelve, a loud knock sounded at the front door. Startled, everyone jumped up from their chairs and hurried into the hall.

"Everyone stay here while I see who's out there," instructed the headmaster.

Nurse Effie stood back with the children. All eyes were on the great wooden doors.

Oddfellow Bluebeard drew himself up to his full height and unlatched the door. He cracked it open and peered out. "Hmph," he muttered. He threw open the door.

They all stared out the door and saw what the headmaster saw.

And what was there? A wild-eyed vagabond? A stray bear looking for hospitality? No. As far as they could tell, it was nothing but the black night sky.

"Strange!" said the headmaster, slowly closing the door. Just before it latched, Delia saw something on the ground. She ran forward and caught the door.

"Did you catch a glimpse of a New Year's ghost, Miss Delia?" Oddfellow Bluebeard joked. Daniel went to help Delia pull the heavy door back open.

When Delia bent down, everyone saw it on the ground: without the traditional basket, or even a blanket, there sat a small baby. It sniffled and shivered in its light cotton nightshirt.

"Oh, my! It's Baby New Year!" exclaimed Oddfellow Bluebeard.

The baby's cheeks were chapped from the cold. It blinked up at the figures crowding into the warmly lit doorway.

Nurse Effie gently picked the baby up and brought it inside.

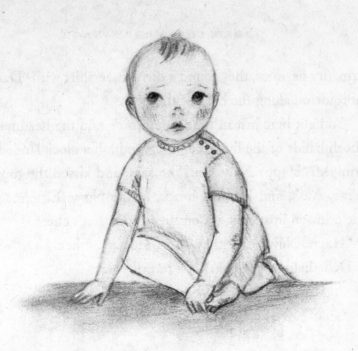

The baby looked around with interest. Delia stroked its little feet as Nurse Effie brought it into the living room. Ava gathered blankets that were thrown over the backs of the chairs and couches, and made a soft mound on the couch. Nurse Effie laid the little creature down on the nest of blankets.

Delia smiled and clambered up on the couch next to the baby. *I'm not the newest one here anymore,* she thought. The baby grabbed her thumb. "Welcome, little one," Delia said with her eyes.

Daniel was sent to fetch baby clothes and a diaper from the laundry room closet. When Nurse Effie changed the baby into warm, dry pajamas, they found a dirty undershirt with "Davey" embroidered along the back of the neck.

"You got here just in time, young sir!" said the headmaster as both hands of the living room's grandfather clock landed on midnight. "Happy New Year!" he said, and kissed the tops of Delia's, Ava's, and Daniel's heads, before Nurse Effie made a little crimson lipstick mark on the headmaster's cheek.

"Happy New Year!" they all said to each other.

Delia held up her notebook to everyone.

Nurse Effie picked the baby up again, and everyone oohed over his rosy cheeks and his cute tuft of downy hair. At that moment, anyone standing outside Oddfellow's Orphanage would have seen in the golden light of the living room something that looked very much like an ordinary family: a tall man with a blue-black beard, two little girls, a boy in glasses, and a lady dressed in white, holding a squirming baby.

ON New Year's morning, the rest of the house stirred into motion, welcoming the tiny newcomer into a family that was hardly ordinary, but rather . . . extraordinary. A family stitched together from the scraps of other families, living together in the enormous house made of brick that is called Oddfellow's Orphanage.

ACKNOWLEDGMENTS

Thank you kindly:

To my editor, Mallory Loehr, for her clever head and lovely heart. Her curiosity about this band of ragamuffins, and the hospitality she showed them, helped grow some scrappy seedlings into a garden of stories.

To Nicole de las Heras, designer extraordinaire, for her beautiful work, impeccable eye, and love of dancing bears.

To the rest of the Random House team, for taking such good care of this book.

To my agent, Brenda Bowen, for lending me her warmth, expertise, and kind words.

To the lace in my shoe, Josiah, for listening to the orphans' stories from the beginning, when they were but little urchins.

For granting me access to your magnificent mind. For being so good to me.

To A. and the three fairies, for always being game for chats concerning important things like sea monsters, orphans, and cake.

To the other A., for lending her uncommon eyes and stalwart encouragement.

To F., for the support and sweetness and light.

To my friends living here with me among the giant firs, and those scattered to the four winds.

And

To my family, who formed the underpinnings for so much about these stories, in ways both obscured and obvious. This is, perhaps more than anything else, a valentine to you and to the real Oddfellow Bluebeard (whose beard was truly red).

EMILY WINFIELD MARTIN is a story and picture maker. She is fond of rabbits, pies, and seashell-pink poppies. She likes to bake sweet things and hunt for old children's books and 1930s dresses. Emily's work is inspired by fairy tales, vintage children's clothing, old toys, her favorite music, and her own life.

The world of *Oddfellow's* began as a series of portraits of imaginary people, each accompanied by a short tale of how that person came to the orphanage. The series was inspired by many things, chief among them an affinity for orphans and the beautiful, mystical iconography of a fraternal order called the IOOF. The portraits grew into the stories contained in this book: adventures and vignettes taking place in a gentle land of lake monsters and dancing bears that exists in Emily's waking dreams.

Emily lives among giant firs in Portland, Oregon, with her best fellow, Josiah, and her rotten cat, Miette. She runs a cottage industry called the Black Apple, through which she sells her artwork, paper goods, and etceteras. You can find her at emilywinfieldmartin.com.

The text of this book was set in Adobe Caslon. It was designed by Carol Twombly in 1990 and based on William Caslon's original type specimens.

The cover art for this book was painted in acrylic.

The interior art for this book was rendered in graphite.